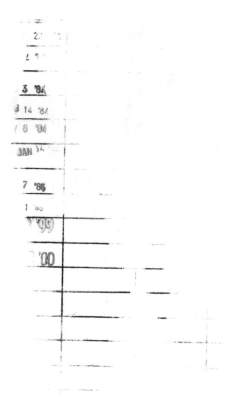

The Mystery in the Secret Club House

by Kal Gezi and Ann Bradford
illustrated by Mina Gow McLean

THE CHILD'S WORLD

ELGIN, ILLINOIS 60120

Library of Congress Cataloging in Publication Data

Gezi, Kal
    The mystery in the secret club house.

    SUMMARY: Upon entering their secret club house, five
youngsters discover they have had a mysterious visitor.
    [1. Robbers and outlaws—Fiction. 2. Mystery and
detective stories] I. Bradford, Ann, joint author.
II. McLean, Mina Gow. III. Title.
PZ7.G33902My   [E]   78-6418
ISBN 0-89565-027-4

Distributed by Childrens Press, 1224 West Van Buren Street, Chicago,
Illinois 60607.

Next door to Tom's house, there was a vacant lot. In the lot,

Tom,

Vern,

Linda,

Barry,

and Maria

had built a secret club house. You could hardly tell it was there, for it looked like a pile of old wood from the outside. The children had even made a secret tunnel to its door.

Just now, Tom was entering the secret tunnel.

"Ow!" he said. "I bumped my head!"

"Be careful! You might ruin the tunnel," Barry said from inside.

"Hurry up!" Tom called. "This bag is heavy!"

"I'll help," said Vern. "You pull and I'll push."

Finally, the three boys got the bag inside the club house. Maria and Linda followed them in. They carried another bag. Then all five stood up. They looked around.

"We're getting lots of cans and bottles," said Maria. "Where will we put them all?"

"We can turn the bottles in for refunds soon," said Tom.

"And sell the cans," said Barry.

"Then we'll have lots of money," said Vern.

"And a whole lot more room," said Maria, laughing.

The children put the new bag of cans in
the corner. They set the bottles in a row on
a shelf. Then they sat down on the boxes
around the table. Maria gave each one an
apple to eat. As they ate, they talked for a
while about how they would spend the
money.

Then Barry said, "I'm thirsty. Look at all those pop bottles! But there's not a drop to drink!"

When they finished their apples, it was time to go home. "See you tomorrow," they said.

The next day, the five children rode their
bicycles along the road. They gathered up
all the pop bottles and cans they found.

The children took the cans and bottles to their club house. When they were inside, they stood up and looked around.

"Something is different," Linda said.

"Yes," said Vern. "The bottles are in different places. They've been moved."

"Barry, did you do that to tease us?" Maria asked.

"Not me," said Barry. "I haven't been here since yesterday. Maybe it was Tom."

"No," said Tom. "I haven't been here either. Maybe a dog got in."

"Maybe," said Vern. "But I don't think so."

The next day, the five children rode their
bicycles again. They found more bottles
and cans and took them to the club house.

Inside, they looked around.

"Things have been moved again," said Tom.

"Yes," said Vern. "And a dog couldn't move bottles like that. Look, they're all right side up."

"Who could have moved them?" asked Linda.

No one knew.

"We have a mystery," said Maria, "right here in our own club house."

Barry picked up one of the bottles. Something rattled inside. "Wait!" he said. "There's something in this bottle."

"You're teasing again," said Linda.

"Look!" Barry tipped the bottle upside down. Out fell a sparkling stone.

"Wow!" Vern said. "That looks like a diamond."

"Do you think it is a real diamond?" Tom asked.

"Of course not," said Linda. "But let's put it in our secret hiding place anyway."

"Good idea," said Barry. "Real hidden treasure." Everyone laughed. Barry hid the sparkling stone.

"It doesn't make sense," said Maria. "Who would bother this club house?"

"And where did that sparkling stone come from?" asked Vern. The children talked and talked about the mystery until it was time to go home.

The next day, the children rode their bicycles again. Again they looked for pop bottles and cans.

"Did you see the news on TV last night?" Vern asked.

"Yes," said Linda. "They told about a jewel robbery. A diamond and lots of other jewels were stolen."

"Hey! Remember the sparkling stone?" Maria asked. "The one Barry found in the bottle?"

"Maybe there are more jewels in our club house!" said Tom.

"Let's go back and find out!" Vern yelled. He turned around and went as fast as he could. The others pedaled after him.

Soon they reached their club house. They started through the secret tunnel.

"Wait," Tom whispered. "I think some-one is inside."

"Listen!" Barry whispered.

They listened. Someone was inside, moving bottles and cans. Then that someone began to come out of the tunnel.

The boys and girls dived behind some boxes. They watched a big man come out. He had a box in his hand.

"Maybe he's the jewel thief," Maria said.

The man turned. He had heard Maria! He saw her behind a box and lunged for her!

"Help!" cried Maria. She grabbed the man's arm and bit him as hard as she could.

"Ow!" the man yelled. Then . . .
Tom grabbed the man's coat . . .
Barry grabbed one arm. . .
Vern grabbed one leg . . .
and Linda grabbed the other leg .

The children pushed the man so hard he had to let Maria go. They pushed him harder still, until he fell down.

Now it was the man's turn to yell, "Help!"

Just then a big car drove around the corner. It was a police car.

"Let me take care of him," the policeman said. He put handcuffs on the man.

"How did you know we needed help?" asked Tom.

"Well," said the policeman, "your mother saw a strange man prowling around your club house, and she called the police. I came as fast as I could."

Just then Tom's mother came up. "Are
you all right?" she asked the children.

"Oh, yes," they said.

"Maybe we caught a jewel thief!" Barry
said.

"Are you teasing?" Tom's mother asked.
The policeman looked interested.

Linda hurried through the tunnel, then came back. "Look at this," she said, holding out the sparkling stone. "We found it in a bottle."

"This is a real diamond!" the policeman exclaimed.

"The man had a box," said Vern. They looked around on the ground.

"Here it is," called Linda.

The policeman looked inside. There were the missing jewels.

"I'm proud of you," Tom's mother said. She gave each child a big hug as the policeman took the man away.

That night, the children watched the news on TV. The newsman told about the jewel thief. He showed a picture of Tom, Linda, Vern, Maria, and Barry.

"These children were brave," he said. "They are very good citizens."

"Well," said Tom, "at least we solved the mystery in our club house."